Unmasking the Devil

Unmasking the Devil

Dramas of Sin and Grace in the
World of Flannery O'Connor

Regis Martin

Sapientia Press
A Division of Ave Maria University Communications
Ypsilanti, MI

Sapientia Press
A Division of Ave Maria University Communications
300 West Forest Avenue
Ypsilanti, Michigan 48197

Printed in the United States of America.

Library of Congress Control Number: 2002107092

ISBN 0-9706106-4-5

The awful thing is that beauty is mysterious as well as terrible. God and the devil are fighting there, and the battlefield is the heart of man.

—F. Dostoyevsky, *The Brothers Karamazov*

My subject in fiction is the action of grace in territory held largely by the devil.

—F. O'Connor, *Mystery and Manners*

The type of mind that can understand good fiction is not necessarily the educated mind, but it is at all times the kind of mind that is willing to have its sense of mystery deepened by contact with reality, and its sense of reality deepened by contact with mystery. Fiction should be both canny and uncanny.... Fiction writing is very seldom a matter of saying things; it is a matter of showing things.... A story that is any good can't be reduced, it can only be expanded. A story is good when you continue to see more and more in it, and when it continues to escape you. In fiction two and two is always more than four....There are two qualities that make fiction. One is the sense of mystery and the other is the sense of manners. You get the manners from the texture of existence that surrounds you .... It is the business of fiction to embody mystery through manners, and mystery is a great embarrassment to the modern mind....

—Flannery O'Connor
Mystery and Manners: Occasional Prose
selected and edited by Sally and Robert Fitzgerald
(New York: Farrar, Straus and Giroux, 1974),
pp. 79, 93, 102, 103, 124.

Once again for Roseanne

• Introduction •

FIFTY YEARS AGO the esteemed literary critic Lionel
Trilling, then professor of English at Columbia College
and frequent contributor of highbrow copy to journals of
fashionable liberal opinion, *traumatized* an earnest and
progressive university crowd on the subject of the relationship between the ideas of democratic liberalism and
the world of creative literature. His thesis? He flat out
denied that any such relationship existed. Well, hardly
enough of one, he allowed, to repay people to read—
much less remember—works of imaginative literature
inspired by the liberal mind.[1]

A startling sort of provocation, one would think, for a
liberal academician of redoubtable reputation to make.
But what a wonderful thesis with which to shatter progressive sensibility and self-confidence! His audience,
men and women besotted by a lifetime of devotion to the
shrines and shibboleths of conventional liberal piety, were
doubtless horrified by Professor Trilling's venture in profanation. And who can blame them? Expecting learned

confirmation of the usual conceits and clichés on which a generation or more of ardent liberal votaries had come to depend, Professor Trilling instead made short work of their most cherished idols. Belief in human perfectibility, for instance, along with the inevitability of societal progress, rational planning, secularism, scientism—the whole boring spectacle, in fact, of unrelieved liberal aspiration—appears to have gone haplessly up in smoke.

In fact, having completely sundered the ideas of liberalism from the life of creative literature as such, Trilling grimly set about his work of demolition, reminding his audience that not a single writer of first-rate fiction had ever emerged, from either the American or European experience, armed with thematic preoccupations even remotely consonant with orthodox liberal thought. Between the deep places of the imagination, those hidden springs of creative memory and experience, and the ideas which typically fire the engines of liberal orthodoxy, there exists, he ruefully noted, only a fatal separation.

Especially shocking, one suspects, is the corollary proposition which Trilling likewise drove home, namely, that the declared enemies of liberalism were the writers precisely from whose ranks had come the greatest literature of the modern period. The finest blooms of twentieth-century literary culture, from prose fiction to poetry to *belles-lettres*—adjudged to be so moreover from secular canons alone—had all issued from artists either wholly innocent of the seductions of ideology, or else openly contemptuous of the whole vaunted liberal superstructure. Luminaries like Marcel Proust, Henry James, James Joyce, D. H. Lawrence, Joseph Conrad, Andre Gide, Franz Kafka, W. B. Yeats, T. S. Eliot, Ezra Pound, Ernest Hemingway, William Faulkner, and F. Scott Fitzgerald (a mere baker's dozen) were not the sort of writers likely to enlist in the workaday street struggles of the Fabian Society, nor to agitate, at a discreet distance, in defense of even the least potty proposal for liberal reform. Can one imagine, for instance, a figure as fastidious as Henry James (of whom it was said that his mind was so fine no idea could possibly violate it) accosting members of Parliament with a fistful of screeds drawn up by Beatrice and Sidney Webb?

Now in attempting to unpuzzle the problem, that is, the staggering aesthetic impoverishment of liberal ideas, Trilling does advert to the possibility that liberalism as such might prove to be the least bit defective. Ah, but it is only the merest velleity, from which he quickly retreats, preferring instead the far more pleasing intuition that what is really required are more liberals in dynamic relation to the ideas they already profess. That, he implies, would at once invigorate the muse sufficient to produce an eminently creative literature. Alas, however, the argument at that point simply breaks down, sailing off into an ideological mist all its own.

The trouble with Trilling, of course, is that he couldn't seem to square his imagined remedy for current liberal ennui, with the sheer devastation of his earlier diagnosis of it. In short, the disease was deadly, and among its victims was literature undeniably of the first order. Interestingly, his failure to do so becomes especially apparent at the very moment in the essay when, confronted with the massive corpus of European and American literature (how he must have longed to distill its informing genius for liberal use!), he suddenly stumbles upon the single lapidary quality which all the great works of the past infallibly possess. It is, he confesses, "that piety which descend(s) from religion because it is most likely to have in it the quality of transcendence which, whether we admit it or not, we expect literature at its best to have."

Bingo. Here the good professor touches the heart of the matter, the nerve center whose transcendent vibrations alone give life and meaning to the art of men. And to be sure, he forlornly confesses, it is a dimension of which liberalism, given its essentially superficial view of the world, remains singularly, embarrassingly bereft.[2]

The chief besetting sin of liberalism, you see, cannot be the fact that men of ideology are often attracted to it. To say that is simply to beg the question about the thing itself. What, then, is distinctive about liberalism as such that invites the charge that it is suspect, indeed, fundamentally false and corrupt? Or that it remains crippled in its capacity to generate a life of the imagination equal to the production of great literature? And here I think the artist and poet have the sense of it when, "passionately dedicated to the search for new 'epiphanies' of beauty," to quote the Pope's moving salutation from his *Letter To Artists*,[3] they necessarily stand athwart the ideologue, whose peculiar affliction is that he cannot see in the ordinary affairs of this world the least intimation of the world to come. And when that nexus breaks down, rupturing a whole series of relations—between eternity and time, grace and the flesh—everything collapses. In short, there is nothing left. "The light that lingered in ordinary things," to recall an image from Karol Wojtyla's own poetry, "like a spark sheltered under the skin of our days"—that light falls completely away. And what is left then? Sheer banalization. However competent his technique, or efficient his productivity, the results are always the same: a world shorn of wonder and beauty. A loss of that depth of "spiritual and religious dimension which," the Pope reminds us, "has been typical of art in its noblest forms in every age." Indeed, he tells us, quoting Dostoyevsky, " 'beauty will save the world.' Beauty is the key to the mystery and a call to transcendence."

So long, therefore, as ideology remains in the saddle, and the liberal humanist shows few signs of having been unhorsed, the realities of time and eternity, nature and grace, history and heaven, will continue to suffer an unreal detachment from the life and art of men. Try to imagine, for example, that such had been the case with, say, T. S. Eliot, probably as implacable a critic of liberal ideology as ever existed. Would not the result have been the complete vaporization of his poetry? Could his *Four Quartets*, the masterwork of twentieth century meditative verse, where the themes and rhythms converge "at the still point of the turning world . . . the point of intersection of the timeless with time," have survived so complete a derangement of sensibility? Where provision is no longer made for the myriad collisions of the Cross with the condition of fallen men, their hunger for God yet driving them to seek glints of His glory strewn about the world He made, man's fate is certain to remain solitary, brutish, and short. Complete destitution, warned Jean Danielou many years ago, is the condition of man left to himself, deprived of the energies of God. Or as Whittaker Chambers once put it in a striking formulation: "I was forty years old, and the father of children, before I knew that charity without the Crucifixion is liberalism."

In assessing these infirmities of ideology, I am often reminded of Evelyn Waugh's inspired reply to the critic Edmund Wilson, who, having dismissed Waugh's novel *Brideshead Revisited* on the grounds that the movements of divine grace in the story were offensive to his sense of liberal decorum, received the following comeuppance: "He was outraged at finding God intruding into my story. [But] I believe that you can only leave God out by making your characters pure abstractions." Abstractions are not the stuff of which stories are made. Leonard Woolf, that drudge of socialist ideology, could not, poor man, have written a single, luminous word of his wife's masterpiece, *To the Lighthouse*.

Frank Sheed, that splendid and tireless man of letters, who with his wife, Maise Ward, practically launched the Catholic literary revival of the thirties and forties, observed once that while "the secular novelist sees what's visible, the Catholic novelist sees what's there." Just so. As a painter will take account of the wind when doing landscapes, so must the writer take account of God and

His grace; otherwise the work will sustain no life at all. Isn't that the sense of it?

Miss Flannery O'Connor, about whom all that follows is written, reminds us that "the chief difference between the novelist who is an orthodox Christian and the novelist who is merely a naturalist is that the Christian novelist lives in a larger universe. He believes that the natural world contains the supernatural." Thus, she insists, "a story that is any good can't be reduced, it can only be expanded. A story is good when you continue to see more and more in it, and when it continues to escape you." In fiction, she concluded with an elegance that defies conventional arithmetic: "two and two is always more than four."[4]

I sometimes wonder, incidentally, whether Lionel Trilling, for all the catholicity of his taste, ever actually knew the subject of this study, or read any of her stories. I say that because just about the time Trilling was issuing his lugubrious report on the poverty of the liberal imagination, this shy young Southerner was already turning out a series of chapters, all of striking and prophetic originality, which would soon become her first novel, *Wise Blood*. The writer Alfred Kazin, whom Trilling almost certainly knew, and who was to become the foremost critic of American literature, knew her well, having met her at Yaddo, a place in Saratoga Springs, New York, where writers and artists are free to live and work for extended periods. Years later in his book *New York Jew*, a series of wonderful reminiscences of his life as a writer and critic, among a number of New York intellectuals of whom Trilling was certainly a charter member, he recalled his earlier appraisal in the most lively and categorical terms: "No fiction writer after the war seemed to me so deep, so severely perfect as Flannery. She would be our classic: I had known that from the day I discovered her stories."[5]

All this brings me to the aim of this little book. It is, as its modest size suggests, strictly limited. Intended both as an act of homage to a writer and human being whom I have long admired, *and* as an attempt to awaken fresh interest in her writings among people for whom she is no longer a household name, the book carries no other pretensions whatsoever. It certainly does not presume to lay the last scholarly stone on the so-called edifice of O'Connor Studies. This accounts, by the way, for the blessed absence of most footnotes, unless where absolutely necessary to establish a reference. Nor is it encumbered with learned lists of other books and monographs and articles on or about her life and work, the so-called secondary sources whose range and number can prove bewildering to the beginner. The fact is, I do not mean this book to become in any way a substitute for the experience of actually sitting down to read her work. That, it seems to me, is far likelier to galvanize the reader than anything that even the most adroit or tireless of exegetes can hope to deliver. If O'Connor's stock were suddenly thus to take off, soaring far above the usual literary sludge (I am thinking of the latest blockbuster from Father Greeley), I should be a very happy man. But to paraphrase a famous line from that Dead Master T. S. Eliot: There are no lost causes because there are no gained causes. We fight to keep something alive rather than in the expectation that it will succeed.[6]

Who knows, maybe an O'Connor revival is simply not meant to be. Maybe the feminist deconstructionists will have co-opted her completely. Either way, it does not finally matter. Redeeming the time is not the business of literature; even the loftiest utterances of the human heart cannot redeem. As W. H. Auden once put it, "In the end, art is small beer." Would the world of politics have been laid out any differently had Homer or Dante or Shakespeare never existed to lend the age a certain loveliness of landscape? Was anything written or said against Adolf Hitler that succeeded in saving great numbers of Jews?

Nevertheless, if the purpose of literature, of telling stories, is to help reveal to man his hidden greatness, what Pascal would call the grandeur and misery of man's soul, then O'Connor's stories will almost certainly be read and remembered. For those at least with eyes to see and ears to hear, a greatness otherwise hidden will surely resonate. It was Faulkner who said it best, upon receiving the Nobel Prize for Literature in 1950, when he defined the task of the artist as attempting "to create out of the materials of the human spirit something which did not exist before." In other words, what the writer sought were "the problems of the human heart in conflict with itself which alone can make good writing because only that is worth writing about, worth the agony and the sweat."

If such is the witness of Flannery O'Connor—"the problems of the human heart in conflict with itself"— and I believe most emphatically that it is so, then let the following stand as one grateful reader's prediction: Flannery O'Connor will surely survive, and prosper, so long as an audience exists animated by the same conflicts of the human heart, and thus capable of being drawn, imaginatively, into the peculiar world she wrote about. It is a hidden place where God and man, grace and freedom, may conspire, by the very weapons of art and story, to aid us fallen yet redeemed souls in taking back the night, wresting control from the Prince of this World. And if not, then it won't matter a whit since the Old Guy will have won anyway.

• Introductory Notes •

1 See the Lionel Trilling essay, "The Meaning of a Literary Idea," a paper delivered at the University of Rochester in 1949, later published in his book, *The Liberal Imagination* (New York: Viking Press, 1950), pp. 272–293.

2 Ibid., pp. 291–292. "If we now turn and consider the contemporary literature of America, we see that wherever we can describe it as patently liberal and democratic, we must say that it is not of lasting interest. I do not say that the work which is written to conform to the liberal democratic tradition is of no value but only that we do not incline to return to it, we do not establish it in our minds and affections."

3 Pope John Paul II, *Letter of Pope John II to Artists*, (Boston: Pauline Books & Media, 1999).

4 Flannery O'Connor, "Writing Short Stories," in *Mystery and Manners* (New York: Farrar, Straus & Girioux, 1974), p. 102.

5 Alfred Kazin, *New York Jew* (New York: Syracuse University Press, 1996), p. 204.

6 Eliot wrote that way back in 1930, by the way, in an essay titled "Notes After Lambeth," which went on to make the point, perhaps more apocalyptic now than ever, that

the world "is trying the experiment of attempting to form a civilized but non-Christian mentality. The experiment will fail; but we must be very patient in awaiting its collapse; meanwhile redeeming the time; so that the Faith may be preserved alive through the dark ages before us; to renew and rebuild civilization, and save the world from suicide."

· 1 ·

HER LIFE BORE such startling and sustained eloquence of pain that when finally she left it, (August 3, 1964) one would be hard-pressed to find another writer of comparable stature with which to compare her. Indeed, as one admiring critic put it—in a comparison wholly without hyperbole—she summoned the voice of Sophocles, an artist whose vision had likewise reached down into the dark places of the human heart, there to reveal with "all the truth and all the craft . . . man's fall and his dishonor."[1]

Flannery O'Connor has been dead longer than the young people I now teach have been alive—students, many of whom have never even heard of her—and the weight of her reputation remains as fixed as Faulkner's (whom, alas, they have not heard of either). This is a remarkable achievement for a writer whose body of published work amounts to only a couple of novels and a handful of short stories. The achievement is altogether astonishing, however, in light of her last years, the fourteen or so of which she spent dying of disseminated

lupus. A rare and terrible disease, its cumulative debili-
ties failed utterly to diminish either the grace of her
spirit or the beauty of her art. "All my life," she was
wont to say, "death and suffering have been brothers to
my imagination."

Acceptance of her end would seem thus to have
come fairly early. It could hardly have come easily. For all
the brave talk of brotherhood, is any ever possible with
enemies as fearsome as these? Amid the ruinous terms of
this world, death remains the ultimate evil, and in every
brush with suffering, even the most fleeting, there is
always some foreshadowing, some showing of the skull
beneath the skin. Nevertheless, she steeled herself to
accept both suffering and death, serenely acquiescing to
whatever losses each in turn would exact. Always she
sought *passive diminishment*, that condition of suffering
whose meaning she had first learned from Pere Teilhard
de Chardin, who doubtless had seized upon it in the writings of the Apostle Paul, who learned it from Jesus
Christ. And its chief lesson? That one ought cheerfully to
endure every affliction one hasn't the capacity to escape.
All this she set about doing because, as with the sufferings of Christ, the terrible diminishment of *His* cross,
such sufferings bring to those who have borne them well
a triumph and consummation not unlike His own. It is
nothing less than the Christian life itself, pressed to the
point of starkest analogical extremity—without, however, any correlative loss of freedom or hope. On the contrary, there accrues such enlargement of soul and personality that grace alone may account for it; of such grace

the sheer outpouring exists in complete, scandalous disproportion to the data of one's own crushing debility.

It was early winter 1950 and O'Connor had been staying with friends in Connecticut. There, intent on the discipline of her work, a novel (her first) slowly began to take shape. Suddenly she fell ill. Subsequent diagnosis revealed the worst: symptoms identical to those which, exactly ten years before, conspired to kill her father. She thereupon returned to Georgia, to her mother's farm, Andalusia, located outside the town of Milledgeville where she had grown up and gone to college. It was here she elected to remain to the end, fourteen years away. Here she would get her dying done every day.

Nowhere else, I think, is the testimony of this extraordinary woman more compelling, more completely self-disclosing, than in her published correspondence: more than six hundred pages issued in 1979 by her longtime friend, Sally Fitzgerald, who rightly has called it *The Habit of Being*.[2] Edited with superb sensitivity and grace, the letters provide the most luminous revelations of a soul absolutely determined on centering everything in Christ, including especially the terrible illness of her own body.

People inevitably ask: what sort of soul had she, this acute and remarkable woman of our time, who managed, despite all its dissociated sensibility, to actually *feel* life from the standpoint of the central Christian mystery: that it has, for all its horror, been found by God to be worth dying for?[3] Who was this pious creature, if you please, of the institutional and hierarchical Church, who yet could advance arguments on behalf of its paradoxical mystery as brilliant as anything from Boussuet to Bernanos? Who was this thoroughly modern woman whose life and work riveted not upon gestures of neurotic feminist defiance against an alleged patriarchy oppressing her spirit, but upon a sacramental vision everywhere validated by its teachings? "The Catholic sacramental view of life," she wrote, "is one that sustains and supports at every turn the vision that the storyteller must have if he is going to write fiction of any depth."[4] Like Jean Danielou, the marvelous and incisive French Jesuit who loved best of all that Church "mud-splashed from history" because finally it was Christ Himself covered with all the muck and the mire of human mortality, Flannery O'Connor's romance with Roman Catholicism remained perfectly ardent and uncomplicated right to the end.[5]

Who—the question persists—was she? What was she really like, this doomed Southerner of nearly thirty-nine years, dying nine days before her birthday (the same age, as it happens, as Pascal, whose intensity she brings to mind), among whose stories are to be found the finest blooms of American fiction? Who was this strangely blithe, wonderfully self-possessed women, in whose letters, says Sally Fitzgerald, "we cannot fail to see the increase in her own being, commensurate with and integrally related to her growth in stature as a writer"? If, as Mrs. Fitzgerald suggests, the correspondence constitutes an aspect of her life very nearly quintessential, that is, a being whose *habitus* of growth the letters meticulously record, what then are the characteristic features, the defining lines, the lineaments as it were, of her soul?

"There she stands, to me," recollects Mrs. Fitzgerald in her moving Introduction, "a phoenix risen from her own words: calm, slow, funny, courteous, both modest and very sure of herself, intense, sharply penetrating, devout but never pietistic, downright, occasionally fierce, and honest in a way that restores honor to the word."

The letters begin at age twenty-three, and they continue with the most wonderful regularity, verve, and wit until almost the end when, six days before her death in an Atlanta hospital, they suddenly ceased. Whatever their worth as literature, and that appears undeniably high, it is the evidence they present concerning the quality of her soul that principally commends them to us. "I have come to think," writes Mrs. Fitzgerald, "that the true likeness will be painted by herself, a self-portrait in words, to be found in her letters...." Reading through them, she confesses to having "felt (Flannery's) living presence" throughout. "Their tone, their content, and even the number and range of those she corresponded with, revealed the vivid life in her, and much of the quality of a personality often badly guessed at." Even the ravages of disease, so obvious, for instance, from photographs taken at the time, seem at once to vanish in the light of something more. "Her letters wipe them all away, not in a cosmetic sense certainly, but by means of something that lay within...."

For example, to playwright Mary at Lee, with whom a friendship of deep affection and mutual devotion was to develop, she sent off this account of her illness, the tone at once bantering and slam-bang:

> You didn't know I had a Dread Disease didj'a? Well I got one. My father died of the same stuff at 44 but the scientists hope to keep me here until I am 96. I owe my existence and cheerful countenance to the pituitary glands of thousands of pigs butchered daily in Chicago, Illinois, at the Armour packing plant.

To another friend, though, she will strike a very different note; it is, by turns, both rueful and humorous:

> I have never been anywhere but sick. In a sense sickness is a place, more instructive than a long trip to Europe, and it's always a place where nobody can follow. Sickness before death is a very appropriate thing and I think those who don't have it miss one of God's mercies. Success is almost as isolating and nothing points out vanity as well.... I come from a family where the only emotion respectable to show is irritation. In some this tendency produces hives, in others literature, in me both.

Or this, finally, from a letter to the poet Robert Lowell and his wife, whom she had first met and admired in

New York in the late forties; it surely reveals something of what must have lain within:

> I am making out fine in spite of any conflicting stories. I have a disease called lupus and I take a medicine called ACTH and I manage well enough to live with both. Lupus is one of those things in the rheumatic department; it comes and goes. When it comes I retire and when it goes I venture forth. My father had it some twelve or fifteen years ago but at that time there was nothing for it but the undertaker; now it can be controlled with the ACTH. I have enough energy to write with and as that is all I have any business doing anyhow, I can with one eye squinted take it all as a blessing. What you have to measure out, you come to observe closer, or so I tell myself.

Such a telling sentence to end with: "What you have to measure out, you come to observe closer...." Not, heaven knows, a measuring in any Prufrockian fashion: the weary aesthete emptying out his life with so many discretely measured coffee spoons. O'Connor may have been under sentence of death, but it was not *ennui* that would kill her. How well, then, the sentence succeeds in telescoping that quality of her life and work which to this day remains so incisive, so incandescent. It is exactly that which so moved the monk Thomas Merton, on the occasion of her death, to write her name with honor, to pronounce that when he read her he remembered, "not Hemingway, or Katherine Anne Porter, or Sartre, but rather someone like Sophocles. What more can you say for a writer?" Here, by anyone's reckoning, is an inventory of human character altogether arresting. How difficult it is to imagine anyone this side of sanctity at all worthy of it. Certainly from among the current fraternity of arts and letters, distressingly few examples leap to mind. With the possible exception of Walker Percy, whose death in 1990 silenced a voice of distinctive Catholic resonance, I cannot think of a single American writer whose passing has inspired anything remotely lapidary.

The late Miss O'Connor was clearly someone of special distinction, perhaps even of blessedness. And not, I would want to insist, at this or that high moment either, between which lay long stretches of unrelieved mediocrity. "Not the intense moment," writes T. S. Eliot near the end of "East Coker,"

> Isolated, with no before and after,
> But a lifetime burning in every
> moment....

What must have threaded all her moments, stitching everything into place, was courage, a virtue not much in evidence these days, particularly among writers and politicians, for whom the absence of valor is a distinguishing mark. Yet there is the uncommon quality, the unending, unvanquished capacity for the one thing needed, the one condition upon which literally everything else in the moral life must depend. "What shall I say of fortitude," asks St. Bruno, founder of the Carthusians, "without which neither wisdom nor justice is worth anything? Fortitude is never conquered; if it is conquered it is not fortitude."

In the absence of this virtue, wisdom tells us, and experience confirms the telling, no other virtue will do because none can survive the moment of real crisis, of testing, without it. At such moments virtue itself must put on courage, else all enactment will fail for want of resolution. "For most of us," continues Eliot in "The Dry Salvages,"

> This is the aim
> Never here to be realized;
> Who are only undefeated
> Because we have gone on trying....

It is courage alone on which the human task of trying, again and again, completely to realize sanctity— "Never here to be realized"—is mounted in the human heart, the sincerity of its ascent to God dependent upon this most necessary of virtues.

And as always, ineluctably, there stands in the midst of each man's struggle, each effort of soul to have or hold integrity, the Evil One. He remains the one, Miss O'Connor unhesitatingly believed, against whom all salvation is at risk, no greater human drama than which can ever exist. It is the decisive human drama, which is destined to be played out somewhere in this world by everyone in this world. A world, moreover, in which a myriad of fallen angels, despite Christ's definitive work of Redemption, remain at large, more than ever holding their own. Athwart the Evil One, she insisted, who is not "simply generalized evil, but an evil intelligence determined on its own supremacy," the indispensable weapon will be courage.[6]

Who else but the Devil, then, deserves the first word in the titanic struggle of human liberty to configure itself to truth, to that web of grace whose meaning bears the name of Christ? Surely the "Old Guy" achieved his masterstroke sometime in the nineteenth century when he managed to persuade huge numbers of people to stop believing in him. Once that ruse got around—and, as always, educated opinion was most eager to help it along—the Devil was at liberty to do his worst. What becomes of sin in a world suddenly divested of belief in an Evil Intelligence bent on bedeviling us with its false attractions? The lust of the eye and of the flesh, the pride of life, these omnipresent dangers of which the New Testament record speaks, are precisely the result of sin, of the primordial catastrophe and its aftermath which overtook our First Parents in the Garden of Paradise. The whole complex structure of the moral law inevitably collapses once the scaffolding of sin (hence virtue), is removed.

And certainly he has returned the favor vouchsafed him by the nineteenth century, for the twentieth century bears unmistakably the imprint of iniquities not of this world. Without doubt the bloodiest century on record, we simply cannot attribute all our horrors and futilities to mere human agency. As Monsignor Ronald Knox wryly put it, "It is so stupid of modern civilization to have given up believing in the devil when he is the only explanation of it."

The world and the flesh having thus fallen on both his and Adam's account, it would seem that the recovery of a healthy sense of sin absolutely depends on getting everyone to believe, once more, in the Devil, that is, in the existence of such powerful and personalized evil as to be able to explain the fact of a wickedness both widespread and intractable. Otherwise, of course, we augment the aims of the Old Guy, whose current ploy of concealment works to his advantage and not ours. This is especially the case where the figure of Evil is given comic form, as witness any number of Hollywood movies. Who is going to ascribe real existence to a being thus transformed into farce, burlesque? "If any faint suspicion of your existence begins to arise in his mind," advises C. S. Lewis' wily Uncle Screwtape to his nephew Wormwood, "suggest to him a picture of something in red tights, and persuade him that since he cannot believe in that (it is an old textbook method of confusing them) he therefore cannot believe in you." Dressed as a harlequin, however minatory the look of the pitchfork, he is hardly likely to inspire terror. And yet, as Pope Paul VI well knew, he remains "the number one enemy, the source of all temptation...the sophistical perverter of man's moral equipoise, the malicious seducer who knows how to penetrate us (through the senses, the imagination, desire, utopian logic or disordered social contacts) in order to spread error...."

And if such testimony were not eloquent enough, particularly from a pope, the tragedy of whose final days was that he felt "the smoke of Satan" within even the Temple of God itself, Holy Scripture reminds us that the whole world is under the power of the Evil One, who is not called the "Prince of this world" for nothing. Think only of our Lord's ordeal in the desert: If the Devil offered Christ all the kingdoms of the earth in exchange for His submission, then perhaps it was because he was in a position to dispose of them.

So, I say, let the Devil have his due, but no more. If the first word is his, let all the rest belong to God, who in His Word broke Satan's sham kingdom in two.[7]

Notwithstanding the victory wrought by God's Word, whose Speech is pure, unending Salvation, we necessarily face, now and for the duration of this world at least, the Dragon. (Others, alas, may face him forever!) Determined on the complete ruin of man and his world, he stands against all that God created, which, simply because it exists as created, God declares it from moment to moment to be good. Contingent, yes. A child of poverty, to be sure. Defiled even by sin. But in God's eyes a thing of goodness, a place of delight. This no doubt helps explain the peculiar and undying malice of the Dragon. He remains the very one against whom St. Cyril of Jerusalem warned the Children of Light, besieged then by the Arian darkness engulfing the fourth century (a period, incidentally, full of alarming and instructive parallels to our own).

"The Dragon," he wrote to the catechumens of Jerusalem, "is by the side of the road, watching those who pass. Beware lest he devour you. We go to the Father of Souls, but it is necessary to pass by the Dragon."

Infinitely wise words, O'Connor fashioned them for "the dark city where," she notes with dismay, "the children of God lay sleeping," undisturbed by the moral ebb and flow of their own lives. The words are meant to awaken, and thus to mobilize, all in whom the drama of salvation has grown dim. Those countless unrecollected souls, for instance, whom the poet Eliot had in mind in *The Wasteland*, where, at the end of the first movement, "The Burial of the Dead," he writes:

> Unreal City, under the brown fog of a winter dawn,
> a crowd flowed over London Bridge, so many,
> I had not thought death had undone so many.

If, as some wag once put it, there are three kinds of people—those who make things happen, others who merely watch while it happens, and, finally, those who wonder what happens—it is pretty clear what camp O'Connor had in mind for the denizens of her dark city. And, of course, nothing ever really happens to them save death and the judgment of nullity that follows. How can Heaven welcome into its precincts of felicity souls so little possessed of joy or zest as to leave no impression at all upon the world they left?

So resonant and prophetic, in fact, did O'Connor find Saint Cyril's warning that she made a point of placing it right at the beginning of her first collection of stories, *A Good Man is Hard to Find* (1955), which she thereupon dedicated to her friends Sally and Robert Fitzgerald. "Nine stories about original sin, with my compliments," she said simply. They are wonderful to behold. Meeting every expectation of their author's ambitious send-off, they conspire on every page to edify and delight. So many fictional lives spent in flagrant defiance of Almighty God, lived in arrant and repeated flight from His laws; then, all at once, startled and overtaken by a primitive violence divinely calculated to shake even the most hardened habitual sinner. It is the complacent heart, after all, the soul unmoved by its own misery, its own lack of love, that renders the creature most resistant to grace. Once inflicted, however, the violence invariably moves the character to an encounter with grace, with judgment, which is then either accepted or rejected. Shorn of all pretense, all duplicity of self, the soul suddenly finds itself confronted by "an action or gesture both totally right and totally unexpected," says O'Connor, "a gesture which somehow makes contact with mystery."[8]

But mystery has been the great hobgoblin of the modern age. We fear and abhor it because we can neither calculate its coming nor control its content. It simply happens. Like an unexpected gale force wind blowing across the benign surface of a backwater bay, it sweeps all life before it. We cannot anticipate its advance anymore than we can assess its impact, the unexpected devastation left in its wake. In short, its unscheduled appearance upsets the best laid plans of nerdy little men bent on rationalist schemes of perfection.

Yet, at the same time, mystery remains the chief medium in which God moves; all that He is and everything He's about reeks of the unaccountable, of the sheer inscrutability of His plans. If, to cite the famous patristic paradox, you thought you understood God, it would not be God whom you had understood. If the things of God were somehow within the reach of man, how then could we say that the Higher Power, God, was beyond our world? The God whose very name bespeaks being, who remains the infinitely impenetrable I AM WHO AM of Exodus 3, is not reducible to so many snug categories beloved by Cartesian minds. He will not allow Himself, in Fr. John Courtney Murray's wonderful summary of a thousand years of apophatic theology, to be "crowded into a concept." Perhaps this is why we moderns prefer the numerical to the numinous; at least we can control the numbers, or so we tell ourselves.[9]

Accordingly, many readers may find the resulting mystery and grotesquerie of an O'Connor story more than ordinary flesh and blood can bear; recoiling in fastidious horror, for instance, from an opening story whose lurid telling requires six murders in less than twenty pages. (Good heavens! And eight more stories left to tell. . . .) For such squeamish folk, O'Connor offered the following ingenious defense: "Violence is a force which can be used for good or evil, and among other things taken by it is the Kingdom of Heaven. But regardless of what can be taken by it, the man in the violent situation reveals those qualities...which are all he will have to take into eternity with him."[10]

And so, while the encounter with the Dragon remains an abhorrent and unwelcome one for both character and reader alike, it forms the key to unlocking the secrets of God's own strategy, which alone bring healing and salvation to man. It is, in fact, what makes the story itself work, driving the energy of the tale; it is the thing that enables it to rivet the attention of the reader, plunging his mind and heart into that vast and mysterious sea of the divine life and our participation in it, to wit, to the plane of anagogy, whence the deepest realities unfold.[11]

Of this encounter with violence, with the Dragon— including both the responsibility of the writer truthfully to evoke it and that of the reader vicariously (at least!) to face it—O'Connor had this to say:

> No matter what form the dragon may take, it is of this mysterious passage past him, or into his jaws, that stories of any depth will always be concerned to tell, and this being the case it requires consider-able courage at anytime, in any country, not to turn away from the story-teller.

· 2 ·

LET US NOT TURN AWAY, then, and gathering our wits and our courage, let us have a look at one or two of her stories, representative specimens as it were, in order to see something of the fierce and necessary confrontation they offer with the sinister and fearful figure of the Dragon. Determined as she obviously was on waging total war against sentimental aberration in whatever form—that being among the chief stratagems of Satan in our time—O'Connor certainly succeeded in routing a good deal of it, and with the most amazing salutary thoroughness in all her stories. But of these, far and away the most searing must surely be "A Good Man Is Hard To Find," the lead story in the collection of the same name. It is the *locus classicus* of her fiction, and the one probably more widely anthologized than any other; manifestly it remains the most vividly remembered of her tales. Whenever she was invited to speak, she would, as often as not, horrify her listeners by reading this story to them. She did this for reasons which are perfectly, if fearfully plain: namely, that the story's central character, the Misfit, is a figure of incomparable savagery and lucid perversity.

The story, in starkest outline, is as follows. A family of five, plus a silly old grandmother with a cat called Pitty Sing, set out for Florida in a car that, thanks to the vagaries of the old woman, overturns in a ditch, leaving them prey to the Misfit, a strange homicidal maniac who methodically sets about killing everyone. That, drastically truncated, is the story. However, the details are steeped in the deepest irony since the Misfit turns out to have been the Good Man of the story's title! Why is that? Because notwithstanding a life wickedly misspent (hence the misfit of the name), he is the only character in whom, to recall a phrase from Francois Mauriac (whom O'Connor greatly admired), "the utilization of sin by grace" achieves final and concentrated expression.

What is meant by that? Simply put, the story aims to show the reader how the virulence of his poison might become, in the hands of a supremely ironic God, medicine for another's salvation. At the last, grace-charged moment before blasting the culpably silly grandmother to God—the weight of whose Judgment she is far likelier to survive, the Misfit having blessedly purged her of all sentimental dross—he tells her that Jesus was the only One that ever raised the dead, and He shouldn't have done it.

> "He thrown everything off balance. If He did what
> He said, then it's nothing for you to do but throw
> away everything and follow Him, and if He didn't,

then it's nothing for you to do but enjoy the few minutes you got left the best way you can—by killing somebody or burning down his house or doing some other meanness to him. No pleasure but meanness," he said and his voice had become almost a snarl.

Whereupon the old lady, her mind suddenly fuzzy with fear, mumbles, "Maybe He didn't raise the dead." To this blasphemous disavowal of divinity, however much driven by an understandable terror of death, the Misfit replies, "I wasn't there so I can't say He didn't."

"I wish I had of been there," he said, hitting the ground with his fist. "It ain't right I wasn't there because if I had of been there I would of known and I wouldn't be like I am now."

His voice close to cracking, obsessed by a knowledge he cannot possess, a faith he will not profess, the grandmother's head momentarily clears. Seeing the twisted face so near to her own, so near to tears, she suddenly cries out, "Why you're one of my babies. You're one of my own children!"

She reached out and touched him on the shoulder. The Misfit sprang back as if a snake had bitten him and shot her three times through the chest. Then he put his gun down on the ground and took off his glasses and began to clean them.

"I have found," wrote O'Connor in an essay furnishing the perfect footnote to the pistol report, "that violence is strangely capable of returning my characters to reality and preparing them to accept their moment of grace. Their heads are so hard that almost nothing else will do the work. This idea" she continues, "that reality is something to which we must be returned at considerable cost, is one which is seldom understood by the casual reader, but it is one which is implicit in the Christian view of the world."

The heads of readers, no less, need returning to reality, to that bedrock realization upon which all human reason and sanity depend. One of the sadder aspects of our fallen condition is the fact that too often the truth of things will only leave an impression—conformity to that reality to which we must be returned—when the precipitating agent is violence. When, quite suddenly, our own tidy, well-supplied worlds come crashing to pieces, we are forced for the first time to see what illusions we have built upon.

I am reminded of a lapidary line from William McNamara's *The Human Adventure*,[12] a splendid book exhorting a life of contemplation for everyone. A stunning sentence, it rudely strips away all sentimental assurance that we are somehow a religiously renewed people, who have wonderfully succeeded in making a place for God. "HE IS," thunders Father McNamara, "THE PLACE OF THE WORLD!" God's coming into our world, in other words, is less like the appointed appearance of a doddering old aunt with whom now and again we sip tea than like a neutron bomb going off in the broom closet; it rips apart the place we thought was ours, along with the idea that there could ever be a safe place to store the Lord of the Universe.

The problem here is one of knowing just how to handle people—characters and readers alike—whose habitual tendency is one of thoughtlessly viewing even the starkest of deformations in the world and in themselves as part of the natural order of the universe, the customary furniture, as it were, of a perfectly laid out cosmos. When, on the contrary, the whole point of the story—the point, in fact, of the writer's vocation as a Christian—is to show that none of it is the least bit natural at all. We live and move amid a fallen and corrupt world, the impacted structures of whose deformity Christ came to dismantle and destroy. Only then may He re-clothe our shattered selves in innocence and joy.

"When you can assume that your audience holds the same beliefs you do," O'Connor argues, " you can relax a little and use more normal means of talking to it." But when they are at variance? Ah, then you must make your vision as shockingly evident as craft and conviction allow. "To the hard of hearing," she observes, "you shout, and for the almost blind you draw large and startling figures."

Not unlike those wonderfully graphic billboards whose sudden and recurrent appearance along highways of otherwise barren secularity have caused a certain ripple of curiosity. Where do they come from? Who has paid for them? Could (gasp!) God actually have written them? Three of my favorites are: "We need to talk." "Will the road you're on get you to My place?" "Great Wedding. Can I Come to the Marriage?" All are signed, of course, by God.

The mood of a "A Good Man..." fairly crackles with tension. It is anything but relaxed. As for the means O'Connor uses to talk to her audience, I should think the speech with which the Misfit concludes the story a pretty fair specimen of the author's own style, direct and pulverizing as a pistol shot. "She would have been a good woman," the Misfit says of the Grandmother, in that wonderful dialect he has, "if it had been somebody there to shoot her every minute of her life."

In the first story, an unreal world sentimentalized into being by a silly old woman has to be shot completely to pieces before grace can deliver her soul from Hell. In the second, "The River", an equally unreal world, rather than simply be smashed, is instead abruptly forsaken by a little boy named Bevel, who plunges headlong into a stream whose swift current, he believes, will wash him onto the shores of Heaven. Unlike the cloying grandmother blown to glory by bullets, Bevel's deliverance involves death by drowning, an event precipitated by the perverse and ironic figure of Mr. Paradise, a piglike man who comes after him brandishing a foot-long stick of peppermint. (O'Connor was not averse to striking the frequent comic note, as witness Mr. Paradise, or, for that matter, the hilarious if unwitting use of a psychopathic killer, who talks like a theologian, to do the work of God.)

The world Bevel is fleeing from is one where nothing ever matters and nobody ever counts; an unredeemed world whose essential emptiness he cannot express but, deep down, feels driven somehow to escape. Rescue takes the form of a backwoods preacher, who introduces him to a very different world, at once luminous and superior to anything he has known before. It is a world whose sublime point of entry begins in Baptism, the vestibule of the life to come. "Maybe I know why you come," he tells the crowd gathered at the riverbank to watch. "Maybe I don't."

If you ain't come for Jesus, you ain't come for me. If you just come to see can you leave your pain in the river, you ain't come for Jesus. Listen to what I got to say, you people! There ain't but one river and that's the River of Life, made out of Jesus' blood. That's the river you have to lay your pain in, in the River of Faith, in the River of Life, in the River of Love, in the rich red river of Jesus' Blood, you people! All the rivers come from that one River and go back to it like it was the ocean sea and if you believe, you can lay your pain in that River and get rid of it because that's the River that was made to carry sin. It's a River full of pain itself, pain itself, moving toward the Kingdom of Christ, to be washed away, slow, you people, slow as this here old red water river round my feet....I read in Mark about an unclean man. I read in Luke about a blind man. I read in John about a dead man! Oh you people hear! The same blood that makes this River red, made that leper clean, made that blind man stare, made that dead man leap! You people with trouble, lay it in that River of Blood, lay it in that River of Pain, and watch it move toward the Kingdom of Christ.

The preacher invites young Bevel to lay his burden of pain and sin in the blood red river, then watch it move toward the Kingdom of Christ. "Have you ever been Baptized?" he asks. "What's that?" murmurs Bevel, unaware of the central rite of Christian initiation, the pivotal moment in anchoring a man's life to God. "If I Baptize you," the preacher tells him, "you'll be able to go to the Kingdom of Christ. You'll be washed in the river of suffering, son, and you'll go by the deep river of life. Do you want that?" Clearly the boy does, in his inchoate longing for something more to life than the loveless comforts of home, and so the preacher, turning him upside down, holds the startled child's head under the water while he says the words setting him free, elevating him at last into the Kingdom of Christ. "You count now," he tells him. "You didn't even count before."

But later that night and the following day, amid the usual disorders and oppressions of a home where plainly he does not count, the boy resolves to return to the river and finish the job. "He intended not to fool with preach-ers any more but to Baptize himself and to keep on going this time until he found the Kingdom of Christ in the river." And so, putting his head under the water he pushes off in the direction of the welcoming depths downstream. But the water will not have him, and so he flails against the stream until hearing a shout and turning his head to look, he sees "something like a giant pig bounding after him, shaking a red and white club and shouting." It is Mr. Paradise come to do him violence. At the sight of him, the boy finds himself suddenly drawn deeper into the water and this time, says O'Connor, "the waiting current caught him like a long gentle hand and pulled him swiftly forward and down."

> For an instant he was overcome with surprise; then since he was moving quickly and knew that he was getting somewhere, all his fury and fear left him.

The story ends with the pig-like Mr. Paradise, his head appearing from time to time on the water's surface, casting about in futile search for the boy. "Finally, far downstream, the old man rose like some ancient water monster and stood empty-handed, staring with his dull eyes as far down the river line as he could see." Bevel, meanwhile, thrust deep down into the river, its swiftly moving current sweeping him far from the frivolous and unreal world he left behind, has—who can doubt?—gone home to God, to the real Paradise where all men count.

· 3 ·

ASKED WHY so many Southern writers, herself in particular, felt drawn to writing about freaks, Flannery O'Connor answered simply, "Because we're still able to recognize one."

> To be able to recognize a freak you have to have
> some conception of the whole man, and in the
> South the general conception of man is still, in the
> main, theological ....While the South is hardly
> Christ-centered, it is most certainly Christ
> haunted. The Southerner who isn't convinced of it,
> is very much afraid that he may have been formed
> in the image and likeness of God ....It is when the
> freak can be sensed as a figure for our essential dis-
> placement that he attains some depth in literature.

Of all the O'Connor stories, there is one in which the
presence of the freak is especially persuasive and dramatic,
his symbolization of human displacement harrowingly

true and exact. It is the final story of her first collection and, not surprisingly, she called it "The Displaced Person," the very title conscripted, as it were, to adumbrate a theme, universal in its application. Leaving aside the figure of the old priest, so delightfully dotty as regards the accidents of being, so gimlet-eyed as regards the essentials (oh yes, and the peacocks!), everyone in the story is a freak of the most lethal and appalling proportions. The real irony, of course, is that it reveals how those least willing to confess it will, in due course, exhibit the most frightful freakishness of all.

Mrs. Shortley, for instance, whose proud ascent we observe at the very outset of the story—"up the road to the hill where she meant to stand," from which prominence "she might have been the giant wife of the countryside, come out at some sign of danger to see what the trouble was"—foreshadows a descent of the most terrifying humiliation and death at the end. In other words, having ascended falsely and too soon, she is doomed to fall. And so, like Tiresias, we watch, while "on two tremendous legs, with the grand self-confidence of a mountain," she stands, watching as the lone black car carrying priest and displaced family arrive to set grimly in motion all the Sophoclean drama of her undoing. Poor Mrs. Shortley "had never given much thought to the devil for she felt that religion was essentially for those people who didn't have the brains to avoid evil without it." She is about (i.e., *shortly*) to experience such profound estrangement from grace and truth that even the most ordinary and habitual contours of her life and world will uproot and displace her. It will leave her seared at the last with the terrible knowledge of her own folly and limitation, forced "to contemplate for the first time the tremendous frontiers of her true country."[13]

Or Mrs. McIntryre, the beleaguered widow who owns the farm to which the displaced persons from Poland have come to live and work: She, too, is destined for displacement. Although greatly delighted at first by their arrival ("at last I'm saved!"..."One fellow's misery is the other fellow's gain." "That fellow is my salvation!"), she soon grows mightily impatient and weary of their foreign ways, in the end confessing regularly her exasperation to the priest-sponsor. He, of course, remains persistently bemused, his attentions fixed by turns on the peacocks ("What a beauti-ful bir-drrd!"), and Purgatory, concerning which he tirelessly spends afternoon visits catechizing Mrs. McIntryre, "while she squints furiously at him from an opposite chair." Interrupting one such lesson, she blurts out, "Listen! I'm not theological I'm practical! I want to talk to you about something practical!" His reverie shattered, she proceeds at intemperate length to unburden her mind about one of the Poles, telling each bead of her disapproval, a veritable rosary of alleged shortcomings of her "salvation."

> He turned then and looked her in the face. "He has nowhere to go." he said. Then he said, "Dear lady, I know you well enough to know you wouldn't turn him out for a trifle!" And without waiting for an

answer, he raised his hand and gave her his blessing in a rumbling voice.

She smiled angrily and said, "I didn't create his situation of course."

The priest let his eyes wander toward the birds. They had reached the middle of the lawn. The cock stopped suddenly and curving his neck backward, he raised his tail and spread it with a shimmering timorous noise. Tiers of small pregnant suns floated in a green-gold haze over his head. The priest stood transfixed, his jaw slack. Mrs. McIntyre wondered where she had ever seen such an idiotic old man. "Christ will come like that!" he said in a loud gay voice and wiped his hand over his mouth and stood there, gaping.

Mrs. McIntryre's face assumed a set puritanical expression and she reddened. Christ in the conversation embarrassed her the way sex had her mother. "It is not my responsibility that Mr. Guizac has nowhere to go." she said. "I don't find myself responsible for all the extra people in the world."

The old man didn't seem to hear her. His attention was fixed on the cock, who was taking minute steps backward, his head against the spread tail. "The Transfiguration," he murmured. She had no idea what he was talking about. "Mr. Guizac didn't have to come in the first place," she said, giving him a hard look.

The cock lowered his tail and began to pick grass. "He didn't have to come in the first place," she repeated, emphasizing each word.

The old man smiled absently. "He came to redeem us," he said and blandly reached for her hand and shook it and said he must go.[14]

The conflict, unmistakably, of priest and Pole pitted against Mrs. McIntyre, while most real and protracted, is one to which the latter is simply not equal. For all her aggressive posturing about the Pole's unworthiness and ingratitude, her need to be rid of him no matter how vaunted his efficiency ("He's extra and he's upset the balance around here...and I'm a logical practical woman and there are no ovens here and no camps and no Christ Our Lord," who incidentally, "was just another D. P. [displaced person]"), Mrs. McIntyre cannot bring herself directly to fire him. Instead, events conspire to produce their own resolution, leaving her beneficiary of a choice she had not chosen directly but willed, nonetheless and implicitly, to her lasting sorrow....

What happens is this. Mr. Shortley, back to work following his wife's untimely death, sullen and resentful at his employer's manifest failure to turn out the Pole, undertakes to poison the well of local opinion against her. Finally, unable to bear the increasing guilt, she moves purposefully toward the machine shed where the men are readying the tractor for work, prepared at last to let the D. P. go. Mr. Guizac is under the tractor intent on some repair or other; Mr. Shortley, meanwhile, is backing another, larger tractor out of the shed.

He had headed it toward the smaller tractor but he braked it on a slight incline and jumped off and turned back toward the shed. Mrs. McIntyre was looking fixedly at Mr. Guziac's legs lying flat on the ground now. She heard the brake on the large tractor skip and, looking up, she saw it move forward, calculating its own path. Later she remembered she had seen the Negro jump silently out of the way as if a spring in the earth had released him and that she had seen Mr. Shortley turn his head with incredible slowness and stare silently over his shoulder and that she had started to shout to the Displaced Person but that she had not. She had felt her eyes and Mr. Shortley's eyes and the Negro's eyes come together in one look that froze them in collusion forever, and she had heard the noise that the Pole made as the tractor wheel broke his backbone. The two men ran forward to help and she fainted.

Resolution is swift and inexorable, leaving no doubt about its outcome of displacement. By sundown her help is gone and, stricken shortly thereafter with nervous affliction, she is forced to sell the farm.

A numbness developed in one of her legs and her hands and head began to jiggle and eventually she had to stay in bed all the time with only one colored woman to wait on her. Her eyesight grew steadily worse and she lost her voice altogether. Not many people remembered to come out to the country to see her except the old priest. He came regularly once a week with a bag of breadcrumbs and, after he had fed these to the peacock, he would come in and sit by the side of her bed and explain the doctrines of the Church.

As always in any O'Connor story, there is more to this one than even its final, sweeping displacement of those characters whom sin has drawn to doom. We, too, are meant to be drawn, if not literally to doom, then certainly to some imagined condition thereof. All her stories, to the extent they succeed at all, are meant to impart an analogous ordeal of judgment: one the sobering point of which should remind the sinner (surely the widest possible bond among readers?) what precisely are the wages to be paid. Thus the stories work to fix the attention upon that which remains essential, what matters most in the moral life, namely that we have souls to save or lose for all eternity. O'Connor forces the reader to see that reality which, amid the smooth sentimental surface of most people's lives, might otherwise never be seen.

Of all the effronteries of the age, surely the hardest for the Christian to bear are those which issue out of his imagined self-sufficiency; that perfectly ludicrous conceit, implicit in much of science and technology and all of the contrived structures of secularity, that man, having finally come of age in the twentieth century, no longer requires the reactionary superstitions of antique religion to shore up his world. Never mind, of course, the fact that the twentieth century was the most bloody-minded century in history, an age whose numberless death camps will put to shame anything from Nero to the nineteenth century. Ours is unquestionably an age whose future prospects, despite an exuberant material prosperity, appear (even to the prosperous) unrelievedly bleak and unwelcome. If, to paraphrase Orwell, one wants a picture of the future, imagine then a jackboot, stamping upon a human face forever. Imagine 1984: a world in which provisions for institutionalized terror are so vast and systemic that not even the least impulses of human love are permitted to survive.[15]

"If you will not have God," warned T. S. Eliot, "and He is a jealous God, then pay your respects to Hitler and Stalin." Even at its antiseptic best, ours is a world wrapped in cellophane. Can it not be a good thing, now and again, to pierce the cellophane?

The situation of displacement, then, to the degree it forces us to face facts, is a mighty salutary thing. We are, just to begin with the most sundering fact, not of this world, hence we can have no enduring place in it. "We seek the city that is to come," the Scriptures tell us. We can have no lasting place here below. Whether real or simply imagined, the experience of being displaced, uprooted from all we had once thought our own, including ourselves, can, like the certainty of being hanged in a fortnight, most wonderfully concentrate the mind. It tends to arrest and draw the self back to first questions: To bedrock, to contingent being, maybe even to God, Whom, never much in our needing before, had gone mostly unnoticed. Until now.

· 4 ·

IN THINKING OF THIS GALLANT WOMAN, who
died almost as many years ago as she had lived, one has
the sense that in her stories—stories in which the most
harrowing passages of literature are construed, countless
passages both past and into the jaws of the Beast—she
reveals far more of herself than simply her craft; she bares
something of her soul, which is every bit as compact of
mystery and struggle, God and the Devil, as may be found
in even the strangest scenes of her books. This, I submit,
is as it should be. How could it be otherwise with human
beings? We are creatures shaped, after all, almost entirely
by our choices, which is to say, by ourselves. Heaven and
Hell are not merely states of being on the far side of history; they are here and now, amid the details of quotidian
life. "Everything nudges our elbow," notes Tom Howard in
The Novels of Charles Williams. "Heaven and Hell seem to
lurk under every bush. The sarcastic lift of an eyebrow
carries the seed of murder, since it bespeaks my wish to
diminish someone else's existence."

Whatever the complex mix of freedom and grace in this vale of soul making, and ultimately the equation can never resolve itself arithmetically, however hard the theologians work to unpuzzle it, we remain essentially responsible beings before God for all that we do. God, after all, long ago paid our race, in C. S. Lewis's phrase, "the intolerable compliment" of taking our liberties with utmost seriousness.[16] We are, in other words, finally and forever what we do, and those changes wrought in us by what we do, whether for good or for ill, can best be understood in the light of what some have insisted on calling character. For example, Francois Mauriac, who probably shaped as much as anyone could from a distance the contours of Miss O'Connor's character, has this to say on the subject: "Just as there is a close bond between a man's character and what happens to him during his life, so there is a similar relationship between a novelist's character and the creatures and events brought into being by his imagination." (Hence the need, as Mauriac put it, always to "purify the source.")[17]

What then were the exact contours of Flannery O'Connor's imagination, her character, in a word, her soul? What was it that finally lay behind so manifest and abundant a display of courage? That mysterious something which lay within? Was it her faith, her attachment to which certainly burned most fiercely and fundamentally all her days? In this connection one recalls with intense pleasure the reply she gave Mary McCarthy, the lapsed Catholic, who thought the Eucharist at the very least an interesting symbol. "If its just a symbol," thundered Flannery, "then the Hell with it!" What an icebreaker that must have been....

"Her intellectual and spiritual taproot," as Mrs. Fitzgerald called it, "deepened and spread outward in her with the years." How marvelously articulate it made her, too. "I see," she once wrote, "from the standpoint of Christian orthodoxy. This means that for me the meaning of life is centered on our Redemption by Christ and what I see in the world I see in its relation to that." The formulation is certainly characteristic of her style, with its intransigent insistence on the need for Christ—"the ragged figure," she called him in her first novel, *Wise Blood*, "who moves from tree to tree in the back of [Hazel Motes'] mind." A strange and prophetic figure, she limned his character in such a way that his integrity absolutely depended on his inability ever to rid himself of that ragged figure. "That belief in Christ is to some a matter of life and death has been a stumbling block for readers who would prefer to think it a matter of no great consequence," she wrote in 1962 when, after ten years, the novel was re-issued.

How, then, to account for her hero? What were his ultimate concerns, the finalities that drove him? For O'Connor, as for the Church whose teachings she never felt the least need to apologize for or deviate from, the basic question, the consuming question, was always the same: Where do we stand in relation to Christ? To the Event of the Cross? Will we be found facing the Wood, our hands clasping the bloody feet like the holy women of Jerusalem, clinging with all our might to the pierced and crucified figure on whom the world's salvation depends? Or will we remain instead in perpetual, neurotic flight from the Cross, putting as much distance as possible between us and It? I shudder to recall the mordant remark once made by the writer J. F. Powers, that in the end great numbers of Catholics may be found at the foot of the Cross immersed in a game of bingo. Indeed, like the soldiers dicing for the clothes they had just divested Jesus of, huge busloads of the faithful may be found parked along the periphery of Golgotha, wholly indifferent to the Drama unfolding before them. But for O'Connor, and the characters she sculpted out of the rough and simple stone of her region, Christ would remain the centerpiece, the linch-pin, without whom nothing mattered and no man was saved. And so, like Hazel's grandfather the circuit preacher, "a waspish old man who had ridden over three counties with Jesus hidden in his head like a stinger," O'Connor placed her considerable skills as an artist at the service of Christ, on whom she drew again and again to cauterize her audience with the saving truths of His Gospel.

In this sense, it is well to remember that she both thought and wrote like St. Augustine and all those oth-ers steeped in the tradition of the Desert Fathers of the early Church. What I mean by the comparison is that while wedded to the things of God, she remained con-tinually and acutely conscious of her own historical moment as well, of which the salient feature, then as now, seemed to her to be an accelerating descent into barbarism. It is that peculiar state of darkness in which despite the utter absence of light, no one appears to have noticed the enveloping night. In other words, a civilization must surely have undergone a final relapse into barbarism when, notwithstanding the surrounding gloom, people persist in the strange pretense of putting on a mask of mirth as if, cavorting like harlequins at a costume ball, they all expected to awake basking in a midday sun. The evidence of collapse and disintegration are all about them, yet they will affect not to notice the rot. Nihilism without the abyss, someone has called it. Actually, it is a kind of despair, only domesticated in order not to render the ordeal of it unendurable.[18]

O'Connor, however, wasted very little time lamenting the state of culture. What today we would call increasing levels of toxicity served only to sharpen, for her, the ancient distinctions: distinctions between the redeemed City of God, the unseen borders of which it became the Church's business everywhere to extend, and the degenerate City of Man, whose boundaries, alas, belong anywhere in this world. On that sundering basis, she saw the Church as really the only credible instrument of salvation around: a sacramental reality quite sufficient to elevate all that is human, through Christ, back to the Father, who intended the world for glory from the first instant His Spirit breathed it into being. Is that not the sense Augustine had in mind when, describing the Church he loved so well, he called her *mundus reconciliatus ecclesia* (The Church is the world reconciled)? Or Gregory of Nyssa, his Eastern counterpart, exclaiming: "The foundation of the Church is the creation of a new universe. In her, according to the words of Isaiah, new heavens and a new earth are created; in her is formed another man, in the image of Him who created him." In short, the Church remains the last best hope of humankind; she is, in de Lubac's incisive phrase, "the sheltering womb and matrix of the new world."[19] And just as Christ calls the world to enter into the Church, His appointed Ark of Salvation, so too does He command the Church to enter into the world, piercing it right to the heart in order thus to raise it all to the awesome dignity of a sacrament. Let the following excerpt from a letter written in 1955 suggest something of O'Connor's intense certitude concerning the sheer salvific importance of the Church, this Mater et Magistra whom God Himself paradoxically intended to be the instrumental cause of the world's salvation:

> I think that the Church is the only thing that is going to make the terrible world we are coming to endurable; the only thing that makes the Church endurable is that it is somehow the body of Christ and that on this we are fed. It seems to be a fact that you have to suffer as much from the Church as for it but if you believe in the divinity of Christ, you have to cherish the world at the same time that you struggle to endure it.

Under the circumstances, it is scarcely surprising to learn that she made, on Fitzgerald's showing, "a striking apologist for Catholicism, which was," she adds, "an arguable system of belief and thought to many, even most, of the people she wrote to." (Or for, for that matter.) "One of the awful things about writing when you are a Christian," O'Connor confessed at one point (with what exasperation we may well imagine), "is that for you the ultimate reality is the Incarnation, the present reality is the Incarnation, and nobody believes in the Incarnation. My audience," she intuited correctly, "are the people who think God is dead."

In the midst, therefore, of all the godless men of modernity, whether they be atheists of the Academy or the Marketplace (the distinction is Fr. John Courtney Murray's, advanced with elegant persuasiveness in his little book, *The Problem of God*), the apostolate of those who emphatically do believe necessarily becomes that of convincing those who do not that both the effort to understand the universe without Him (i.e., the atheist academic), and the will to prosper within it without Him (i.e., the bourgeois atheist), must sooner or later come to grief. A world without God, quite simply, is a world unfit for humanity; it is a world in which men must literally gasp for breath. "The merely human," warned Chesterton, "is inhuman." On that basis, it will move inevitably toward ultimate shipwreck. Man without grace is less than zero.

Now, to be sure, few of us can convince the godless any time with sufficient adequacy to satisfy anyone.

O'Connor, however, could do it over and over again with the most piercing, imaginative brilliance. In short, her preferred way to persuade the godless that God had better not be dead (by the way, is it not a trifle odd to be speaking thus of I AM WHO AM?) was to spin tales which truthfully rendered the consequences of their belief that He was. Here she would unfailingly flesh out for her readers what surely must remain the most ludicrous aspect of our fall from grace, to wit, our persisting and sentimental refusal ever to acknowledge that we had and have.[20]

I think of the huge and hulking figure of Joy, for example, from "Good Country People," a 32 year-old nihilist with a wooden leg (the real one was blown off in a hunting accident when she was ten), "whose constant outrage" reports O'Connor, "had obliterated every expression from her face." Only we mustn't call her Joy, she having changed it to Hulga for reasons both comic and perverse. "She considered the name her personal affair," O'Connor tells us.

> She had arrived at it first purely on the basis of its ugly sound and then the full genius of its fitness had struck her. She had a vision of the name working like the ugly sweating Vulcan who stayed in the furnace and to whom, presumably, the goddess had to come when called. She saw it as the name of her highest creative act. One of her major triumphs was that her mother had not been able to turn her dust into Joy, but the greater one was that she had been able to turn it herself into Hulga.

Not exactly an ideal woman to consort with in even the best of circumstances (which, come to think of it, do not exist in the fictional world of Flannery O'Connor), she wore the look of one willfully determined to remain morally blind. Forever. Hers will be the Great Refusal. And her comeuppance? It is wonderfully and hilariously ironic. In the course of being hoodwinked by an oily and unscrupulous Bible salesman intent on stealing her wooden leg, she finds herself robbed of something far greater: her soul. "I don't have illusions. I'm one of those people who see through to nothing," she breezily tells the bogus Bible salesman as he is about to make off with her leg, not to mention the fatal illusion that she is somehow free of any. And her reaction to so brazen a theft? "Her face was almost purple. 'You're a Christian!' she hissed. 'You're a fine Christian! You're just like them all—say one thing and do another. You're a perfect Christian, you're...." To all of which he loftily replies: "I hope you don't think that I believe in that crap." And turning to leave he contemptuously tells her:

> "And I'll tell you another thing, Hulga," he said,
> using the name as if he didn't think much of it.
> "You ain't so smart. I been believing in nothing
> ever since I was born!"

In an essay titled "Writing Short Stories" that attempts to identify the characteristic challenge facing the author, she writes: "The peculiar problem...is how to make the action he describes reveal as much of the mystery of existence as possible. He has only a short space to do it and he can't do it by statement. He has to do it by showing, not by saying, and by showing the concrete—so that his problem is really how to make the concrete work double time for him." By her own admission, O'Connor certainly intended "Good Country People" to be understood in that way. Plunging beneath the obvious hilarity of the situation, the story succeeds simultaneously in awakening yet another level, the point of insertion being the wooden leg itself. Explaining the symbolism this way, she admits that while the average reader is delighted to see anybody's wooden leg being stolen, it is also necessary to invest the hollowed-out leg with a certain weight of meaning if the reader is to be enticed onto a deeper plane of experience. "Early in the story," she explains, "we're presented with the fact that the Ph.D. is spiritually as well as physically crippled. She believes in nothing but her own belief in nothing, and we perceive that there is a wooden part of her soul that corresponds to her wooden leg." Now none of this, she insists, must ever be stated; we are to infer the connection, she assures us, from the texture of things the author has shown us in telling the story. Meanwhile, of course, that old wooden leg continues to collect meaning. "The reader learns how the girl feels about the leg, how the mother feels about it, and how the country woman on the place feels about it; and finally, by the time the Bible salesman comes along, the leg has accumulated so much meaning that it is, as the saying goes, loaded. And when the Bible salesman steals it, the reader realizes that he has taken away part of the girl's personality and has revealed her deeper affliction to her for the first time."

The wooden leg is both literally what it is and figuratively what it is not; that is, a symbol or signpost of something other and more. In tandem, therefore, the two levels become essential to the story's scaffold of meaning. Or, again, on the surface it remains what it is, a sort of primitive prosthetic device, retaining thus the very integrity of the thing itself, that is, the image. But underneath all that, the leg functions equally as a symbol for the corrupt state of Hulga's soul. The vacuity of the unredeemed soul is accordingly prefigured by the hollowness of the wooden leg. And thanks to the weight and compression of that symbol, the story itself expands in the mind of the reader. Or, as O'Connor was fond of saying, in good fiction two plus two is never only four.

In short, to read Flannery O'Connor with an adequacy of attention is, as someone once suggested, on the order of Horatio seeing the ghost of Hamlet's father: "It harrows me with fear and wonder." How well, in other words, she could separate out the sentimental syrup, the cloying treacle of so much contemporary literature, seeing right through to the bone and marrow of real meaning. Not to have understood this, of course, and thus to be pulverized and never quite know why, is the fate of all sentimentalists. The peculiar pestilence of the modern age, O'Connor defined it "as excess, a distortion of sentiment usually in the direction of innocence," that purity of soul we lost a very long time ago.[21]

The shortcoming here is one of sight, of vision, of which the eye, the visual organ, remains the common point of entry to the soul, seat of all moral judgment. "For the writer of fiction," she tells us, "everything has its testing point in the eye, an organ which eventually involves the whole personality and as much of the world as can be got into it." The sin of the sentimentalist is precisely his failure to see that what fundamentally is missing from the moral universe is that very quality of innocence he had falsely attributed to it. The worm in the apple escapes his notice, even as its canker enters deeply into the marrow of the fruit. An instructive example may be the landlady into whose rooming house the self-blinded Hazel Motes has come home to die. Unable to see although nature has endowed her with sight, she is left "staring with her eyes shut, into his eyes," constrained at the very end to feel "as if she had finally got to the beginning of something she couldn't begin," seeing him withdraw ever more into the distance, "farther and farther into the darkness until he was the pinpoint of light." Meanwhile, the motes obscuring his vision have quite fallen away, leaving the course of his atonement triumphant and complete. She of course remains baffled and bedeviled by an outcome for which a lifetime steeped in sentimentality leaves her wholly unprepared.

Here is no harmless habit of which O'Connor speaks, like a preference for watercolors or canasta. Those afflicted with settled sentimental habit can be dangerous folk indeed, particularly when given the power to harness others to illusion. As any trip through a shopping mall will at once tell you, their effusions lie about everywhere. It was Jacques Maritain, on whose book *Art and Scholasticism* O'Connor confessed to having "cut her aesthetic teeth," who declared once that God and the literary artist were agreed to this important extent: while both loved their creations, neither one would ever presume to judge them with sentimentality.

Is the distinction possibly too subtle for the modern world to follow? The modern sensibility—to judge it only by brisk sales in paperback gothic, Rod McKuen, Leo Buscaglia, and Hallmark greeting cards—would appear vastly to prefer a love without any judgment attached to it whatsoever, while remaining absolutely awash with sentiment. How far we have come from Dante who, summarizing a thousand years and more of Christian understanding, spoke of Love as a "Lord of terrible aspect," as well it must be if it is to move the sun and the stars. Or John of the Cross, who knew that in the end each of us would be judged on love—by Love— and who, in saying so, knew perfectly well where this ought to lead the disciple determined on holiness. Or Dostoyevsky, who thought of love's actual content, as distinguished from the superficial syrup, as a most "harsh and dreadful thing."

In *A Memoir of Mary Ann*[22]—a remarkable story about a little girl stricken with cancer, as recounted by the nuns who cared for her (members of a Dominican Congregation begun in the nineteenth century by Rose Hawthorne, "who," O'Connor writes, "were shocked at

nothing and who love life so much that they spend their
own lives making comfortable those who have been pronounced incurable of cancer")—she has this to say about
the noxious fallout from the sentimental:

> One of the tendencies of our age is to use the suf-
> fering of children to discredit the goodness of
> God, and once you have discredited His good-
> ness, you are done with Him. The Almyers whom
> (Nathaniel) Hawthorn saw as a menace have
> multiplied. Busy cutting down human imperfec-
> tion, they are making headway also on the raw
> material of the good. Ivan Karamozov cannot
> believe, as long as one child is in torment;
> Camus' hero cannot accept the divinity of Christ,
> because of the massacre of the innocents. In this
> popular pity, we mark our gain in sensibility and
> our loss in vision. If other ages felt less, they saw
> more, even though they saw with the blind,
> prophetical, unsentimental eye of acceptance,
> which is to say of faith. In the absence of this
> faith now, we govern by tenderness. It is a tender-
> ness which, long since cut off from the person of
> Christ, is wrapped in theory. When tenderness is
> detached from the source of tenderness, its logical
> outcome is terror. It ends in forced-labor camps
> and in the fumes of the gas chamber.

From Almyer to Auschwitz to abortion. Is the distance nearly so far as we thought? Hawthorne's hero

will not abide the least "visible mark of earthly imper-fection," and so he importunes his wife, the merest birthmark upon whose face confounds the idea of per-fection his mind had formed of her, to have it cut out. She is understandably stricken by his words and, burst-ing into tears, exclaims, "You cannot love what shocks you!" No, he cannot. And neither could those adminis-tering Auschwitz. It is, after all, really only a matter of degree, and not that of the kind of shared contempt for imperfect being, which marks the difference between the two. If you can mutilate and kill one person, espe-cially when moved by some lofty and paradigmatic ideal, the problems of liquidating several millions are at best those of engineering, not ethics. And, to be cer-tain, the Almyers have multiplied. Today they run abortion clinics for the poor, whose offspring so offend the current standards of eugenic perfection. Their for-mer Soviet counterparts, meanwhile, once staffed the Gulag, where countless failures of Socialist perfection were sent to their final solution. "Most of us know, now," wrote Randall Jarrell half a century ago, "that Rousseau was wrong: that man, when you knock his chains off, sets up the death camps. Soon we shall know everything the eighteenth century didn't know, and nothing it did, and it will be hard to live with us."[23] Whether Jarrell knew it or not, those chains are an apt symbol for the order of created and redeemed reality, ignorance of which continues to lie at the heart of sentimental disorder. "We lost our innocence in the Fall," O'Connor reminds us, and our return to it is through the Redemption which was brought about by Christ's death and by our slow participation in it. Sentimentality is a skipping of this process in its concrete reality and an early arrival at a mock state of innocence, which strongly suggests its opposite.

· 5 ·

As I say, Flannery O'Connor's stories are hard, diamond hard, but that is only because they are Christian, filled therefore with the hard implacable realism of Christ. "I believe," she once said, "that there are many rough beasts now slouching toward Bethlehem to be born and that I have reported the progress of a few of them."

Such a superbly revealing remark that is. The Yeatsian echo of the line, so startling in its intimation of prophecy, the essential charism, after all, of the storyteller's art, perfectly captures all that is most deeply abiding in her work. She set out simply, and implacably, to see all that was there, her faith the pure light by which she saw. "The Catholic novel," she insisted, "is not necessarily about a Christianized or Catholicized world, but one in which the truth as Christians know it has been used as a light to see the world by." Indeed, the artistry of the Catholic novel is deployed precisely to make known, through the imperfect medium of the art—"for art transcends its limitations only by staying within them"—the truth of all that she had seen.

How otherwise is the writer honestly to fashion stories? By lying? What else save reality has the writer to go on, or to reckon with? Heaven knows, he cannot hallucinate his stories; the craft of fiction is not, after all, chemical. Its proper direction will be toward bedrock, and the beyond, but every quarry begins at eye-level, with whatever is most visibly real. "Fiction operates through the senses," of which, O'Connor would insist, "the first and most obvious characteristic is that it deals with reality through what can be seen, heard, smelt, tasted, and touched." Surely this is why stories appeal so mightily to the sensibility, long before they burrow into the brain.

Whatever the writer sees, therefore,

> must first take on the form of his art and must become embodied in the concrete and human... because every mystery that reaches the human mind, except in the final stages of contemplative prayer, does so by way of the senses.

All this is so—must in fact be so—given the finite and limited nature of all art, most especially the art of fiction, which remains, she never tired of saying, in her hillbilly Thomist way, "the most impure and the most modest and the most human of all the arts...closest to man in his sin and his suffering and his hope."[24]

One recurrent reason why O'Connor's world intrudes so powerfully upon our own, leaving aside here matters of technique and craft—why her images appear so to startle and disturb, their violence so often the instrument of that grace which, when seized upon greedily enough, yields even the Kingdom of Heaven (it suffereth violence, we are told on very good authority, and the violent bear it away)—is that, having herself been there all her life, many times face to face with the Dragon, she knew the mysterious and apocalyptic cast to the human story. "My subject in fiction, " she declared, "is the action of grace in territory held largely by the Devil." And we believe her because, putting it simply, it could not be so in her stories were it not already so in her own story.

O'Connor's life, therefore, constitutes a continuing and compelling theater of instruction; in it we glimpse something of that characterological drama on which depended, besides the confecting of stories, the destiny of her own soul (which, one supposes, subsumes everything else). It is to that stage, then, and to the decisive moments enacted on it, that one ought to turn in order to glimpse her moral style. Without that style the stories she wrote could not exist as they do. In fact, they could never have been written at all but for her character, for its extraordinary capacity to work, as her friend and mentor Caroline Gordon once put it, "within the terrain of the bull." It was courage, before all else, that enabled her to do so.

"The supreme question about a work of art," pronounced James Joyce, "is out of how deep a life it springs." I can think of few other artists of this century who lived more deeply than she did, so utterly at home was she with the great mysteries of her religion. Nor anyone else, for that matter, whose art sprang more directly from life than her own. And I am, for one, profoundly glad that all this should be so. Because I count myself among the most fortunate of readers for having known something of that life and art. For myself, and others similarly blessed, I do not think it an exaggeration to say that we have been vouchsafed that rarest of gifts, the sharing of something precious even beyond price: the truth about ourselves and others, the world and God. It is a truth concerning which many of us have too often forgotten the value. But, thank God, she had not forgotten and, thanks to her, forgetfulness is now that much harder to manage for the rest of us. For myself, certainly—and no doubt for countless others who likewise sin and suffer yet have not ceased to hope—I can never tire of her stories.

How completely her mind and soul found their way into the characters of them! How often one finds great prophets particularly, who stalk the pages of her fiction like so many titans from another time.... Moses, Elijah, Daniel, the Baptizer. In this connection I think often of fierce young Tarwater, hero of her last novel, *The Violent Bear It Away*, "a very minor hymn to the Eucharist," she called it, and only the adjective is wrong (it is far from being minor)—whose hunger at the very end for the Bread of Life, she said, "was so great that he could have eaten all the loaves and fishes after they were multiplied." So, I expect, could she have (and, please God, she is feasting even now).

When Tarwater is summoned at the last—"GO WARN," he is told, "THE CHILDREN OF GOD OF THE TERRIBLE SPEED OF MERCY"—the words are her words, and how perfectly they describe all that she, too, was summoned to do. Her face set, like Tarwater's, "toward the dark city, where the children of God lay sleeping."

From the eulogy preached at the Requiem Mass offered up for her Resurrection, I find these words as moving and true an account of her life as anything I have ever read:

> Truth—the living God—is a terrifying vision, to be faced only by the stout of heart. Flannery O'Connor was such a seer, of stout heart and hope. From her loss we salvage the memory of a "stranger from that violent country where the silence is never broken except to shout the truth." May she rest.

And may her stories, where she shouted out that truth without compromise or surcease, their telling interrupted only by her passing, be marveled at for so long as stories are read, and there are people to read and cherish them with delight.

• End Notes •

1 The reference is to Thomas Merton, from a prose elegy he
wrote in memory of Flannery O'Connor that first appeared
in *Jubilee* magazine in November 1964. It later surfaced in
a collection of his essays called *Raids on the Unspeakable*
(New York: New Directions, 1966).

2 See Flannery O'Connor: *The Habit of Being,* Letters edited
and with an Introduction by Sally Fitzgerald (New York:
Farrar, Straus and Giroux, 1970).

3 "The Catholic writer, insofar as he has the mind of the
Church, will feel life from the standpoint of the central
Christian mystery: that it has, for all its horror, been found
by God to be worth dying for. But this should enlarge, not
narrow, his field of vision." See Flannery O'Connor's essay,
"The Church and the Fiction Writer," *Mystery and Manners* (New York: Farrar, Straus and Giroux, 1974), 146.

4 Ibid., 152. She goes on to make the point, hugely relevant
at this moment of our literary history, that where the
writer fails to attain that depth of imaginative penetration,
it is precisely not the Church that is to blame. Indeed, the
Church, "far from restricting the Catholic writer, generally
provides him with more advantages than he is willing or
able to turn to account, and usually his sorry productions
are a result, not of restrictions that the Church has
imposed, but of restrictions that he has failed to impose on
himself. Freedom is of no use without taste and without

the ordinary competence to follow the particular laws of what we have been given to do." Would that a generation weaned on such solipsism as regularly surfaces among lists of best-selling authors had heeded such sound substantial advice. What a difference an ethos of self-denying discipline can make!

5 In fact, it is what finally enabled her to see reality at all. Her belief in the Church's dogmatic deposit became an essential instrument in determining the extent of her sight. "Christian dogma," she insists, "is about the only thing left in the world that surely guards and respects mystery. The fiction writer is an observer, first, last, and always, but he cannot be an adequate observer unless he is free from uncertainty about what he sees. Those who have no absolute values cannot let the relative remain merely relative; they are always raising it to the level of the absolute. The Catholic fiction writer is entirely free to observe. He feels no call to take on the duties of God or to create a new universe. He feels perfectly free to look at the one we already have and to show exactly what he sees." From Flannery O'Connor's essay, "Catholic Novelists and Their Readers," *Mystery and Manners*, 178.

6 "I have found, in short, from reading my own writing, that my subject in fiction is the action of grace in territory largely held by the devil...I have also found that what I write is read by an audience which puts little stock either in grace or in the devil." See Flannery O'Connor's essay, "On Her Own Work," *Mystery and Manners*, 118.

7 There is, in this connection, a wonderful little story by Graham Greene—in some ways strikingly, thematically akin to O'Connor—called "The Hint of an Explanation," in which a freethinking baker by the name of Blacker attempts to corrupt a young altar boy with literally fiendish cunning. His greed baited with biscuits and toys, the boy is

tempted to turn over to Blacker the holiest thing he knows, the Host, for the profanation of which he has been promised a shiny new train. Only at the last moment does the child, strangely moved by grace, recoil in horror at the prospect of so paltry an exchange.

Greene's point, of course, which he renders with startling and vivid effect, is that evil and damnation do exist, that they are permanent human possibilities, behind which stand sinister, superhuman beings bent on the total subjugation of the soul. Blacker is abject testimony to their success.

How often it is youth, innocence, which serves to inflame the power of darkness—The Thing, Greene calls it—behind the mere human instrument intent on our ruin. Such terrible loss, too, when It appears to have won.

In his haunting poem "Germinal," A. E. (Irish poet George Russell, 1867–1935) writes how, "In ancient shadows and twilights/Where childhood had strayed/The world's great sorrows were born/And its heroes were made/In the lost boyhood of Judas/Christ was betrayed."

8 "There is a moment in every great story," O'Connor writes, "in which the presence of grace can be felt as it waits to be accepted or rejected, even though the reader may not recognize this moment." O'Connor, "On Her Own Work," Mystery and Manners, 118.

9 See his superb and comprehensive study of what he calls "history's most momentous argument," elegantly set out in a series of lectures delivered, of all places, at Yale University. Fr. John Courtney Murray, The Problem of God: Yesterday and Today (New Haven and London: Yale University Press, 1964).

10 Not a few readers and reviewers, by the way, seemed entirely to have missed the point of her stories, the epiphanies of

grace mediated by violence having succeeded rather too well in communicating her distinctive vision. In other words, the message of the supernatural incarnated amid the particulars of time and place appeared so natural, their believability so perfectly evident as it were, that many noticed only the outward violence and missed the meaning altogether. "I am mighty tired of reading reviews that called *A Good Man* brutal and sarcastic," she confessed wearily in 1955. "The stories are hard but they are hard because there is nothing harder or less sentimental than Christian realism....When I see these stories described as horror stories I am always amused because the reviewer always has hold of the wrong horror."

11 "The kind of vision the fiction writer needs to have," O'Connor observes in her essay, "The Nature and Aim of Fiction," (*Mystery and Manners*, 72–73.), "... is called anagogical vision, and that is the kind of vision that is able to see different levels of reality in one image or one situation. The medieval commentators on Scripture found three kinds of meaning in the literal level of the sacred text: one they called allegorical, in which one fact pointed to another; one they called tropological, or moral, which had to do with what should be done; and one they called anagogical, which had to do with the Divine life and our participation in it. Although this was a method applied to biblical exegesis, it was also an attitude toward all of creation, and a way of reading nature which included most possibilities, and I think it is this enlarged view of the human scene that the fiction writer has to cultivate if he is ever going to write stories that have any chance of becoming a permanent part of our literature." And not only the fiction writer. One would surely wish to add the biblical critic as well, for whom too often the meaning of Sacred Scripture becomes an invitation murderously to violate the integrity of God's Word. A kind of "ontological rape"

takes place, to use an expressive phrase my old friend and mentor, Fritz Wilhemsen, would evoke in describing the eviscerations often practiced by modern commentators.

12 William McNamara, O.C.D., *The Human Adventure: Contemplation for Everyman* (Garden City, New York: Doubleday: Image, 1976), 28–29.

13 This image of one's true country, so powerful and arresting, originates in a prayer written by Ernest Hello to the Archangel Raphael, who is God's appointed Guardian sent to lead us to where we need to be; yes, even if to bring us there requires a certain amount of salutary violence. O'Connor admired the prayer very much and said it every day for many years; a copy was found on the table next to her bed in the hospital where she died. It reads:

> O Raphael, lead us toward those we are waiting for, those who are waiting for us: Raphael, Angel of happy meeting, lead us by the hand toward those we are looking for. May all our movements be guided by your Light and transfigured with your Joy. Angel, guide of Tobias, lay the request we now address to you at the feet of Him on whose unveiled Face you are privileged to gaze. Lonely and tired, crushed by the separations and sorrows of life, we feel the need of calling you and of pleading for the protection of your wings, so that we may not be as strangers in the province of joy, all ignorant of the concerns of our country. Remember the weak, you who are strong, you whose home lies beyond the region of thunder, in a land that is always peaceful, always serene and bright with the resplendent glory of God.

14 Note the startling equation, imaginatively struck by the storyteller, between Christ and the character; that is, a

linkage anagogically joining the Incarnate Word, whose coming among us was precisely in order to redeem a fallen human race (and who most emphatically "didn't have to come here in the first place"), to poor Mr. Guizac—who, to be sure, didn't have to come either—but whose mysterious presence in the story so admirably serves the purposes of an ironic and merciful God. Seldom in modern literature does one find so evident and arresting an application of what the Medieval Schoolmen were wont to call the "four-fold method of Biblical exegesis" in which, once again, the author, boring straight through the actualities of the literal text, seizes triumphantly upon the deepest meaning of all, namely the interpenetration of God and man in the Mystery of Christ. As the poet, Hopkins, would exclaim, in lines from a sonnet unmatched for sheer lyric and mystagogic beauty: "... for Christ plays in ten thousand places,/ Lovely in limbs, and lovely in eyes not his/To the Father through the features of men's faces."

15 One thinks of Romano Guardini's *The End of the Modern World* (Chicago: Regnery, 1956), the culminating chapter of which provides one of literature's most haunting lines: "Loneliness in faith will be terrible. Love will disappear from the face of the public world (Matthew 24:12), but the more precious will that love be which flows from one lonely person to another, involving a courage of the heart born from the immediacy of the love of God as it was made known in Christ." Written in 1956, ("begun in the afterglow from the holocaust of the idols of the nineteenth century," to quote from F. Wilhelmsen's incomparably eloquent introduction), it is one of only a handful of books published in the twentieth century which provide seminal and indispensable orientation to post-modern man.

16 "We are bidden to 'put on Christ,' to become like God. That is, whether we like it or not, God intends to give us

what we need, not what we think we want. Once more, we are embarrassed by the intolerable compliment, by too much love, not too little." See C. S. Lewis, *Problem of Pain* (London: Macmillan, 1940), Chapter 3.

17 See Francois Mauriac's moving and heuristic account of the artist's dilemma, which he succinctly sets down in *God and Mammon* (London: Sheed & Ward, 1946), esp. 50–63. He writes, for example: "The ambition of the modern novelist is to apprehend the whole of human nature, including its shifting contradictions. In the world of reality you do not find beautiful souls in the pure state—these are only to be found in ...bad novels. What we call a beautiful character has become beautiful at the cost of a struggle against itself, and this struggle should not stop until the bitter end. The evil which the beautiful character has to overcome in itself and from which it has to sever itself, is a reality which the novelist must account for. If there is a reason for the existence of the novelist on earth it is this: to show the element which holds out against God in the highest and noblest characters—the innermost evils and dissimulations; and also to light up the secret source of sanctity in creatures who seem to have failed" (59). To do this well, says Mauriac, the writer must submit to the counsel of God's humblest priest: "Be pure, become pure, and your work too will have a reflection in heaven. Begin by purifying the source and those who drink of the water cannot be sick..." (63).

18 One is reminded of Kierkegaard's observation, which adorns a lovely novel by Walker Percy, *The Moviegoer*, winner of the 1962 National Book Award: "...the specific character of despair is precisely this: it is unaware of being despair." The quote is from Kierkegaard, *The Sickness Unto Death* (New York: Alfred A. Knopf, 1961).

19 See Henri de Lubac's magnificent (there is no other epi-thet to describe the sheer breathless immensity and grandeur of this work) *The Splendor of the Church* (San Francisco: Ignatius Press, 1986), 170.

20 "What's wrong with the world?"—asked an editorial of its readers around the turn of the century, one of whom was G. K. Chesterton. Readers were duly invited to write in their replies. To which the following was sent: "Dear Sirs: I am. Yours, truly, G. K. Chesterton."

21 This surely accounts for the special advantage borne by the Southern writer, particularly one steeped in Christian con-cerns. For O'Connor, for example, living in a region whose history and memory were inescapably rooted in the defeat and violation of a lost Civil War, this proved enormously simplifying in terms of telling a good story, that is, one fraught with conflict which alone makes for stories of any significant narrative moment. (Who would care to hear sto-ries of a paradisal world without any intimation of our hav-ing once lost it?) "We have had our Fall," she wrote. "We have gone into the modern world with an in-burnt knowl-edge of human limitations and with a sense of mystery which could not have developed in our first state of inno-cence—as it has not sufficiently developed in the rest of our country." Of course, she concedes, the mere fact of losing a war does not create of itself an apparatus of moral sensibility adequate to writing about it, or about anything else for that matter. "But," she says, "we were doubly blessed, not only in our Fall, but in having means to interpret it. Behind our own history, deepening it at every point, has been another history....In the South we have, in however attenuated a form, a vision of Moses' face as he pulverized our idols."

22 See Flannery O'Connor, "A Memoir of Mary Ann," *Mys-tery and Manners*, 213–228.

23 Jarrell's point is strategically placed, that is, a review of Robert Penn Warren's *Brother to Dragons: A Tale in Verse*, consisting of an imaginative re-telling of an atrocious murder of a black slave by the children of Charles and Lucy Lewis, brother-in-law and sister, no less, to Thomas Jefferson, "who," Jarrell acidly comments, "spoke and believed that Noble Lie of man's innocence and perfectability." Randall Jarrell, "On the Underside of the Stone," *Kipling, Auden & Co.* (New York: Farrar, Straus and Giroux, 1980), 177. The poem by Warren, writes Jarrell, "is written out of an awful time, about an awful, a traumatic subject: sin, Original Sin, without any Savior…it wasn't happiness Warren was in pursuit of, but the knowledge of Good and Evil."

24 In good fiction, O'Connor was wont to say, and as I cited several times already, two plus two is always more than four. In other words, it ought to leave some residue of mystery on which the mind and soul might profitably dwell. And it is the meaning of the story which keeps the thing blessedly unbrief. She preferred, she said, "to talk about the meaning of a story rather than the theme of a story. People talk about the theme of a story as if the theme were like string that a sack of chicken feed is tied with. They think that if you can pick out the theme, the way they pick the right thread in the chicken-feed sack, you can rip the story open and feed the chickens. But this is not the way meaning works in fiction. When you can state the theme of a story, when you can separate it from the story itself, then you can be sure the story is not a very good one. The meaning of a story has to be embodied in it, has to be made concrete in it. A story is a way to say something that can't be said in any other way, and it takes every word in the story to say what the meaning is. You tell a story because a statement would be inadequate. When

anybody asks what a story is about, the only proper thing is to tell him to read the story. The meaning of fiction is not abstract meaning but experienced meaning, and the purpose of making statements about the meaning of a story is only to help you to experience that meaning more fully." Flannery O'Connor, "Writing Short Stories," from *Mystery and Manners*, 87–106.